UEA PUBLISHING PROJECT
NORWICH

FRIENDSHIP FOR GROWN-UPS

NAO—COLA YAMAZAKI

TRANSLATED BY POLLY BARTON

Friendship for Grown-Ups
Nao-Cola Yamazaki

Translated from the Japanese by
Polly Barton

First published by
Strangers Press, Norwich, 2017
part of UEA Publishing Project

Distributed by
NBN International

Printed by
Swallowtail Print, Norwich

Series editors
David Karashima
Elmer Luke

Editorial team
Kate Griffin
Nathan Hamilton
Philip Langeskov

Cover design and typesetting
Nigel Aono-Billson
Glen Robinson

Illustration and Design Copyright © Nigel Aono-Billson, 2017

ISBN-13: 978-1911343028

Foreword

"The rock fell into the sea, and became an amoeba…"

So (nearly) begins Nao-Cola Yamazaki's chapbook of three stories, in which many important things seem to be happening at the exact same moment and people exist in entirely contradictory states of being. That rock, from 'A Genealogy', goes through no slow transformation but jolts into a new form, this gargantuan leap from the inert to the biological. When, in another story, an author meets a probing music scholar, she seems to be falling for him, but also not; she is interested in him for her own ambitious purposes, but also not; when a couple, many years broken up, re-gather on a whim to look at the apartment where they once lived, they are at once filled with longing for one another, saddened, happy, relieved, connected, and apart. We live in all of these states, Yamazaki reminds us. We too are rocks and amoebas, in the same second – ancient and rigid, warm and fluid – and once we are an amoeba we will soon surely become something else. The stories engage without solving, allowing a reader access into intimate moments without ever deciding for us what to think. Even when Yamazaki ends a story, which is usually the time a writer reveals her hand, something is left unusually open, something rumbling beneath the words. "It was no longer possible," says writer Terumi, "to separate herself-as-novelist from her true self." And yet. Can she? Will she? Isn't her yearning still palpably there? Is it possible to pinpoint a true self in these exchanges at all?

These stories also feel distinctly of now. Of a time when someone who is around thirty, especially a woman, may feel torn between work and family, or be wondering

how to balance the two, if to balance the two, if
marriage is over as an institution, or if all she might
want is for someone to call her "Teru-chan", unsure if
that option is lost to her forever.

No option is lost forever. The coelacanth, having just
climbed onto the land, looks at the stars and muses to
itself. "As it was thinking, it learned to breathe using
its lungs."

We spend time contemplating one thing, while something
major happens out of our grasp. We morph, and keep going,
and reflect, gain insight and watch as it too slips away.
She pays that very slipperiness, that essence of non-
essence, a beautiful tribute.

Aimee Bender

One day, there was a light. The light hit a rock.

A Genealogy

One day, there was a light. The light hit a rock.

The light filled the rock with life, and it began to produce more amino acids, and grew larger and larger. It grew so large that it became unsteady on its feet, and its body became soft and fluffy, until it could no longer stand on top of its cliff, and toppled off.

The rock fell into the sea, and became an amoeba, and the amoeba began swimming around.

It was quiet in the sea. The only thing the amoeba could hear was the lapping of waves far above, and the bubbling of volcanoes far below.

The amoeba was lonely. It swam for a very long time. For about a thousand years it swam, circling the land endlessly. The reason that I am lonely, the amoeba thought, is that I am totally alone. The amoeba wanted others around.

So the amoeba had sex with itself and made another amoeba. This other amoeba also had sex with itself, and the number of amoeba grew. Soon there were many.

As time went on, the amoeba began to think that maybe sex was not something you were supposed to do by yourself, but rather with others. So it tried attaching itself to another amoeba and having sex that way. And so a child was born.

The amoebas' child grew into a fish, and swam for five million years. The fish didn't only swim in the sea — it swam in the rivers as well.

The fish's child became a coelacanth, and one evening, the coelacanth tried climbing up onto the land. It waggled its fins, and crawled along with a slapping sound.

The moon was full, and there were so many stars that they seemed to fill the whole sky. At that time, there were no towns to give off any light, and so the night sky was bustling with activity.

"The stars are so beautiful! What is a dirty, ugly creature like me doing here under a sky this starry, this magnificent?" The coelacanth folded its fins behind his head and lay back on the rocks, looked up at the sky, and fell into thought. As it was thinking, it learned to breathe using its lungs.

Then the coelacanth laid an egg, and a frog hatched out of it.

The frog gave birth to a dinosaur.

The dinosaur had two boys. The older was a bird, the younger a rat. The younger brother was crafty, and outwitted his older brother. He managed to claim all the land in the world for himself. The younger brother would boast that he been given the land by the gods, and so the older brother, who now had nowhere to go, abandoned the land and took to the sky. The younger brother took over the earth and filled it with his kind, and soon enough, everybody began walking on two legs.

Now that their front legs were freed up, people began to communicate with one another using gestures. In order to tell someone else that something was round, they would make a circular motion with their front legs, and if they wanted to impress on somebody how large something was, they would spread their front legs far apart.

After a time, people didn't feel satisfied by these gestures, and they began to make noises, like "ah" and "oooh". And so, language was born.

Once people had language, they began to give each other names.

Yamada made a living by working in the fields and rearing cattle.

One time, there was a big flood. Yamada got on a boat with a boy and some cows and pets, and for a while they all lived together on the boat. They had a lot of free time on their hands, so they began playing the piano and the guitar. And so music was born.

Yamada had sex with the boy, and they had a child.
They called it Tanaka. Tanaka's parents were always playing
music, and Tanaka grew sick of them. After the water
subsided, Tanaka ran away from home. Tanaka went to live
alone in a cave, and painted on the walls. And so art
was born.

One time, a girl came walking into Tanaka's cave without
asking, and said, "Wow, what's all this!? Did you do these?"

"Mm," Tanaka said, embarrassed.

"You're really good!" the girl said. Tanaka was so happy
at having had the pictures praised by the girl
that they had sex, and then, when they were lying in bed,
they started telling each other stories. And so stories
were born.

Tanaka's child was named Suzuki. Suzuki had five
hundred children.

With five hundred of them now running around, people
started saying that the earth belonged to humans, and
that they could do anything they wanted. This sense of
omnipotence began to spread, and people started building
a tower. When the tower was finished, it was struck by
lightning, and suddenly the five hundred people stopped
being able to communicate with one another. Every one of
them spoke a different language, and people grew estranged
from people who didn't understand what they were saying,
and only people with relatively similar languages would
flirt with one another. As they went about their flirting,
they started establishing countries together.

Each country had its own political system, and was
separated into rulers and slaves.

Most of the slaves in Japan were farmers, and they
grew rice.

Like Yamada who had lived many years earlier, Sato made
a living in the fields. The rice that Sato grew was really
good. Sato lived for 250 years and then died.

Sato's child was called Takahashi. While Takahashi was

alive, Japan ended its period of isolation, and opened its doors to people from foreign nations.

Takahashi gave birth to Itoh. During Itoh's lifetime, the system of fixed social classes was abolished and the number of farmers fell, while the number of people working in the service industry increased. Itoh had nothing to do with the service industry, though — she was a housewife.

Itoh gave birth to Kandagawa. Kandagawa worked in a company. Kandagawa did not have any children. Kandagawa lived in apartment with her boyfriend. Kandagawa threw a red washcloth around her neck like a scarf, and went out with her boyfriend to the public baths in the backstreets. While she was bathing, she stretched out her legs and remembered how, in the past, she used to be a fish. When she looked at the painted nails of her feet that were sticking out of the bathwater, she thought they looked like fins. Kandagawa splashed her feet. She folded her hands behind her head, looked up at the steam, and fell into thought for a while.

The Untouchable Apartment

She opens her eyes and, in the gloom, reaches out to
touch the wall beside the bed. But it does not feel like
she is touching anything. There is no sensation at all.
The wood-effect wallpaper should by all rights feel a little
cool to the touch, but she cannot sense any change in
temperature either. She moves her hand along to touch the
pillar, but it feels neither smooth nor rough.

Kandagawa starts to worry that there is something wrong
with her fingers, and reaches up to touch her face. She can
feel her cheeks. She lifts her hands to the top of her
head, and she can feel her hair.

But when she gets out of bed and crouches down to touch
the wooden floor, she can't feel it. She tries tracing the
joints of the floorboards, but her fingers are just stroking
the air. She is not touching anything.

There are magazines scattered about on the floor, and a
laptop sitting on her desk, but when she goes to pick them
up, they don't move a smidgen.

Out the window she can see a plum tree in bloom, but the
window won't open.

She presses her hand up against the wall once again
and feels nothing at all. Wondering what could possibly be
going on, she pushes her face right up against the wall and
squints to see where the wall and her hand meet. It is then
that she discovers that her hand is about one millimetre
away from the wall. However hard she tries, she cannot get
her hand to meet the surface of the wall. There is no way
to bridge that one-millimetre gap.

Then Kandagawa's eyes opened again. It had been a dream,
she realized, and got up again, pressing her hand to the
wall to check that she was experiencing all the proper
sensations. The bumpy white wallpaper was soft, and a
little warm.

Next, she grabbed the beige curtain that hung near her

bed, and pulled it back. Sunlight came rushing in and lit up her apartment, a far more presentable place than the shabby one in her dream. She opened the window, and cool air flooded in. Feeling the cold, she shut it again straight away.

The apartment in her dream was the place that she used to share with her boyfriend, Mano, now ex-boyfriend. Why was it still there, impinging on her unconscious? She didn't want it there. Kandagawa stretched. She shut the curtain and threw off her pajamas, got in the shower, then went off to work.

Ayumi Kandagawa now lived in a southeast-facing 38-square-metre apartment, complete with an eat-in kitchen and two bedrooms all with laminate flooring, a bathroom with an integrated ventilation and heating system, an automatically locking door, and a secure parcel delivery box, located on the fourth floor of a seven-storey, four-year-old apartment block four minutes' walk from the station, for a monthly rent of 130,000 yen.

At midnight, after getting home from work, Kandagawa was lying on her bed in her pajamas, reading the fashion magazine *Ginza*, when her mobile phone started vibrating. Seeing the name Hideo Mano flash on the screen, Kandagawa didn't feel inclined to pick up. It had been four years since she and Mano had split up. Kandagawa was 31, and she now lived alone.

Three days ago, she had got a missed call from Mano, but she hadn't rung him back. She had no idea why on earth he was calling. They had nothing to talk about. Kandagawa wasn't planning to get married any time soon, but she did have a new boyfriend.

She looked down at her vibrating mobile, weeee, weeee, and when, after six rings, Mano still hadn't given up, she pressed the green button.

"Hello?"

"Kan-chan."

"Are you drunk?"

"Yeah. There was a farewell party for this senior guy at my company. He was really good to me. Taught me loads and loads of stuff."

"Are you walking home?" Kandagawa could hear the sound of traffic on the line.

"Yeah."

"Aren't you freezing? You should've just waited till you got back."

"I don't mind the cold."

Even though they hadn't spoken for four years, Kandagawa had known just by the way that he'd said her name that he'd been drinking. When they were together, he would often call her when he was drunk. She figured that after parting ways with a group he'd been out drinking with, he'd suddenly find himself lonely and wanting to talk to someone. But also, Mano wasn't very good at expressing himself, and he needed a few drinks before he could let himself seek affection from her.

"You know how many years it's been?" she asked.

"Hmm, a really long time, that's for sure."

"Four years. That's how long."

"Wow . . . Your voice is still exactly the same."

Kandagawa and Mano no longer had the sort of relationship where they would just call each other up for no reason.

"So what is it?" said Kandagawa.

"What is what?"

"Why did you call?"

"No particular reason."

"How's work?"

"Same as ever."

"Was it fun, the party?"

"No, it wasn't fun. It's all work people, so I can't really let my guard down."

"Hmm."

THE UNTOUCHABLE APARTMENT

"My boss really likes me though."

"Does he now."

"I've been promoted and everything. They're making me area manager next."

Mano started boasting in the cutesy voice he only ever used when he was drunk. Usually, he spoke more calmly, and with less feeling.

"That's great. Nice going."

"How about you? How's work."

"Not fantastic, really. My head is packed full of all the stuff I have to get done every day, and I feel like I'm always behind."

"Really? That's not like you. Before when I'd call you and ask how you were, you always used to say "I'm good!'"

"Well, I guess I've changed. Become more of an adult or something. Have I gone and disappointed you?

"No."

"So what's your hair like now?"

"A kind of short pudding-bowl thing."

"God, are you serious?"

"You?"

"Mine is kind of fluffy now. I've dyed it brown."

"That's a shame. I really liked your hair before, dead black and dead straight."

"Did you hear Mutoh got married?"

"Yeah."

"He took his wife's name, so now he's Matsumoto. They've had a baby already. I went to his house with Teru-chan to see them a while back. It's a boy. His name's Yoshitomo. He's super-full of energy, he's constantly moving around. His wife has really got her hands full."

"Has she."

"Also, did you know Teru-chan's baby is a model for baby magazines?"

"Nope."

"Her name's Midori. She doesn't look anything like

Teru-chan at all. She's super cute, and really smart too, apparently. Though I don't think anyone can know yet if she's really smart or not since she's still only a baby, but still, Teru-chan insists she is. She seems like she's all set on making sure Midori does really well in school. She's like started talking about entrance exams and things — already! I never thought she'd be the type."

"Marriage is gonna go out of fashion."

"What do you mean by that?"

"I mean, I think that pretty soon, people are going to start thinking of marriage as uncool."

"That time is never going to come. People have always got married, all throughout history. There's never been a time when people didn't marry."

"I'm not gonna."

"It might become fashionable not to legally marry, to have common-law marriages or whatever, but I don't think there will ever be a time when people think it's cool to not have a partner. If that was the trend, the human race would die out."

"Right."

"Really, why did you call me?"

"I just wondered how you were."

"Don't you think it's a bit rude to just drunkenly ring me up?"

"Sorry."

"If you really don't have anything to say, then I've got some work that I want to get done tonight."

"You know, the other day, I visited this place for work that was near our old apartment."

"Really? The apartment with the plum tree." Kandagawa shut her eyes, and she could smell the scent of the tree come drifting toward her. She remembered a tanka she once knew: *when spring blows in, plum tree, let your scent still blossom on the east wind, though I am gone far.*

"I'm not talking about the tree."

"Did you go and see the apartment?"

"Yeah, I kind of felt a bit nostalgic somehow, and wanted to see it."

"Okay..."

"Thing is though... Don't be too shocked, okay?"

"Um, okay?"

"The block has been torn down. It's just a vacant lot now."

"What? No way!"

"I thought you'd be surprised."

"Apartments can just disappear like that?"

"They can."

"Shit."

"Do you want to go see it together?"

"Could."

"Let's. When are you free? What about this Saturday? I know it's short notice."

"Saturday should be fine."

"Okay, shall we meet at the ticket gates at one?"

"Sure."

"Okay. See you then."

"Bye."

Kandagawa was certain that Mano had called her up with the intention of asking her to go and see their old apartment all along. She knew that it was stupid to meet up again with people who you were finished with, but she was bursting with curiosity.

On Saturday, Kandagawa got on a train from her local station to Shibuya, where she changed onto the subway. It was looking like she'd be around a quarter of an hour late, and she sent Mano a message saying so, to which he replied, "OK."

Kandagawa regretted not having the good manners to leave the house in enough time when they were meeting for the first time in ages, and bit her lip as she held onto the train pole, watching the stations pass by. Each station had a platform of a different color — there was a pink one, a yellow one, a pale green one. After a while, the train went above ground. They passed through a residential area, and crossed a river.

She got to the ticket gate at fifteen minutes past one, and called Mano to say that she had arrived.

"I've started walking toward the apartment," Mano said.

"Look, I'm really sorry that I'm late. But why would you go on without me?'

"I dunno. I kind of couldn't believe you'd be late," Mano said quietly.

"Which exit is it again?"

"Shit, another blow."

"Why?"

"Do you really not remember?"

"The one by the university?"

"No."

"The Tokyu exit?"

"Yeah. Look, I'm walking back now, so stay where you are."

"Okay."

If you went out of the ticket gate and turned left, exited from the deserted south exit, and walked a little, you came to the university from where Kandagawa, Mano, and their friends had all graduated. The bustling north exit, which was to the right, had a Tokyu department store right in front of it.

Mano came back almost immediately. He was wearing a suit. He had angular glasses, different from the ones he had worn before. He had put on a little weight. His hair was short all over, as ever, and messy. There was nothing pudding bowl about it whatsoever. He must have been just joking.

"How are you doing?"

"Okay, and you?"

THE UNTOUCHABLE APARTMENT

"Yeah, fine. It really is fluffy isn't it? Have you gone fashionable or something?"

"Shut up, no. Shall we go?"

The two of them began walking.

"Do you really not remember the way to the apartment?"

"It's amazing how easily you can forget those kinds of things. But I remember now. You turn by that bank."

Kandagawa's spatial awareness was not good, and so remembering how to get to places had never been her forte. Back in the day, she had always trusted Mano to take her anywhere they had to go, and, if she got lost when she was out on her own, she would phone him and get him to tell her the way.

"Yeah, that's right."

"Why are you wearing a suit?"

"I had to go to work in the morning."

"Busy, huh."

They had to avoid the bicycles parked on the pavement as they walked along.

"Did you eat lunch yet?"

"No."

"Shall we get something to eat?"

"Sure."

They climbed up the spiral staircase to the Chinese restaurant on the second floor. The waitresses were in white blouses and black skirts, the waiters wore ties, and there were white tablecloths on the tables, but the restaurant wasn't too expensive, and the items on the menu had cute names.

They had come here often. Mano would cycle here from their apartment with Kandagawa perched on the rear rack of his bike.

Kandagawa had bought a bicycle of her own when they'd first moved in, but it had been promptly stolen when she'd left it unlocked in a parking lot one day. From then on, she would walk to the station on the way to work, and get the bus back. If she went out with Mano on weekends, she would piggyback on the back of his bicycle.

On weekdays, Mano would always leave the apartment before her, and get home from work first. If she got home late and missed the last bus, then he would cycle to the station to meet her. One time, she fell asleep on the last train, and woke up two stops further down the line. There was a long queue for taxis. She phoned Mano and he came to get her, and gave her a bike ride the whole two stops' worth.

Both that time and when her bike had been stolen, Mano had moaned at her for being ditzy. He said that it was a waste of time and money, but he had been nice.

"The crispy rice with gravy was good here, wasn't it?"

"Yeah."

"I'd like the 'Piping Hot Ramen', please."

"I'll have the 'Fluffy Fried Rice'," said Mano.

As they ate their meal, Kandagawa said, "I liked the noise that the crispy rice with gravy made."

"You mean the kind of sucking noise when you put the chunks of rice in the gravy?"

"It was a happy noise."

"Yeah."

"I think I'd probably cry if I ate that now."

They walked along a shopping street named after its tulip trees.

The tall trees lined both sides of the street, and small wispy clouds drifted past the yellow leaves fluttering high above their heads.

"It's really cleared up!" said Kandagawa.

"Yeah."

They went past the cram school where Mano had used to work part-time while still at university. Kandagawa hesitated whether to bring this up, but eventually decided not to.

They passed through the shopping street and then began

to walk down the sidewalk of a wide road.

Kandagawa walked on the stone border separating the road from the trees. The border was about thirty centimetres high and she often used to walk on it in the olden days. That way, she was slightly taller than Mano. She used to have him hold her hand as she walked on it as though she was on a balance beam, but now, of course, they did not hold hands. She got down almost immediately. They passed a petrol station, a restaurant, a municipal playing field.

There were some short saw-tooth oaks whose oval leaves, like little fish, were carpeting the road. The leaves crunched underfoot. A purple bus passed them. They took a turn, and passed a dental office, an orthopedic clinic, and a knitting school. Then there was a stretch of detached houses. A lot of them were quite ostentatious, and had all kinds of showy Christmas decorations facing the road.

"They're so pretty!"

Kandagawa pointed to some fairy lights in red and blue, and Mano nodded.

"Yeah."

"Hey, you're less of a misery guts than you used to be."

"I used to get irritated when I looked at those kinds of things. When people placed stuffed toys and things facing out of the window I always wondered why they were looking at me, and feel pissed about it. But now I just think that stuff is kind of cute, I guess."

"That's funny. Hey look, it's a camellia!"

Soft, rich pink flowers stood out against the tough dark-green leaves.

"I still hate flowers, though," Mano said, laughing.

Kandagawa chuckled. She felt suddenly happy, though she wasn't sure why.

At the fork in the road, they took the road leading to the right, and then they reached where their apartment

used to be. Exactly as Mano had said, there was just a
vacant lot there now.

"Wow."

The only thing standing was a sign propped up in the
corner. The rest was just freshly dug earth. The plum tree
was gone. Mano and Kandagawa stepped into the lot.

From their apartment, which had been a bit up a hill,
they had been able to see down to the adjacent town. The
apartment itself had been shabby, but the view was good. In
the town, people were going about the business of living
their lives. It was made up of single-family houses and
apartment blocks. There was a red electricity pylon far off
in the distance, and beyond you could see the outline of
the mountains. There were times when sunlight descended
from the clouds like an angel's ladder. At times, they
had got carried away and had sex with the windows still
open. Kandagawa stood on the soil and looked at the scene
in front of her. From here, things appeared at a gentler
angle than they had from the second floor.

"It was around here, wasn't it, our room?"

"Yeah."

"I'm gonna take a stone to keep."

"Me too."

The two of them crouched down a small distance away
from one another and each chose a stone for themselves.
Kandagawa found a suitably sized one, and put it in her
coat pocket. It looked like Mano also selected a
smallish one.

"Do you think this is uncool, to do this?" Mano asked.

"I don't really care," said Kandagawa. "Let's have this as
an uncool day."

"Okay. How about we buy something from the bakery we
used to go to and eat it in the park?"

"Okay."

She knew the place Mano meant - a natural yeast bakery
at the bottom of the hill, run by a married couple who

had quit their office jobs in order to open up their own business. Kandagawa brushed the soil off her skirt, then stood up.

When they got back to the fork in the road, Mano said quietly,

"I suppose there's no chance of picking up a taxi around here."

"Huh? Why would you want one?"

"I dunno, I just feel tired."

"Is your work that busy?"

"Yeah."

"Really? Is it really tough?"

"Yeah, pretty much. I'm on edge the whole time."

"Oh come on, let's walk."

"Really? Recently, money's the one thing I'm not short of, so I always just catch a taxi everywhere."

"Shit."

Before, Mano never got tired, even when he walked for hours. However long he rode his bicycle, he would still have a grin on his face. But Mano no longer had those manly arms that had used to grip the handlebars. He had probably developed a different kind of muscle in their place, which gave him the strength to get along well with people, but Kandagawa missed those slender, powerful arms he used to have.

They walked down the hill, across the road that led through the vegetable fields, and into the residential area where the small bakery was. They picked out a doughnut and a bun with *hijiki* in it. Mano had bought lunch, and so Kandagawa paid this time.

Then they carried their purchases to the park, and sat on seats fashioned from tree stumps. They halved the bun and the doughnut, and shared them.

"Since we're here anyway, we might as well visit the university," Kandagawa said.

Mano nodded. So then they left the park and set off in

the direction of the university.

"It's tiring, isn't it, all this walking," Mano said, looking toward the road.

"Are you serious?"

"I wonder if there'll be any taxis." Mano brought up the subject again.

"You've gotta be kidding!" Kandagawa felt dejected. She'd never heard the Mano of before even utter the word "taxi."

"You don't want to get a taxi?" said Mano.

"No!" said Kandagawa, firmly. They walked all the way to the university.

The area around the university had changed a lot. Before it had been just fields, car parks, and small shops, but now there was a shopping mall with all kinds of upmarket retailers. They walked past the mall and into the university, where they saw a large LCD screen announcing lecture cancellations and found a computer where you could access all kinds of information by scanning your student card. Everything had gone high tech. When Kandagawa and Mano had been there, everything had been done by paper.

Come to think about it, Kandagawa had started university when she was eighteen, which meant thirteen years had already passed. It was thirteen years, too, since she'd first met Mano.

After using the toilet, they went into a university building and walked down the corridor. One of the classrooms had its door open, so they were able to catch a glimpse of a class taking place. A boy and a girl were making some kind of presentation. The boy was writing something on the blackboard, and the girl was standing, nervously reading something from a sheet of paper. They looked so young. Kandagawa and Mano must have been like that too, at some point, though it was hard to think that now.

They took the stairs downstairs to the basement level.

The university was built on a slope, so they could exit on one side of the building from there.

A path, known as Cherry Lane, stretched a distance from there. The name came from the row of cherry trees that lined the street and that was spectacular in the spring. Now, though, there were but a bunch of withered red leaves, trembling in the wind.

"Let's walk the path. And then call it a day?"

"Okay."

"I guess we're never going to see the cherry blossoms together again," said Kandagawa.

Mano replied straightforwardly, "No, I guess not."

From the station, Kandagawa and Mano would be taking the same train as far as Shibuya.

The platform had been rebuilt, so it was sparkling and new. There was no sign of the dull stone wall that had been there before.

The platform used to be at the bottom of a steep cliff, with a stone wall above waist height separating the two. Mano would jump up and sit on the wall while they were waiting for a train, like he was jumping up onto a vaulting horse.

They let two local trains go past, then got on the express. As soon as they got in the train, Mano looked about for a free seat and sat down. Kandagawa sat next to him. Mano put his briefcase on his knees, and took out a young men's magazine. The fluidity of his movements made Kandagawa realize that this must be his routine coming home from work every day. Still, she was pretty amazed that he was still reading *Young* magazine. There were some magazines that she would have understood, like *Morning*, which she herself liked and often read, but she couldn't believe that this was something that someone of Mano's age could still enjoy.

"Do you want to read this with me?" Mano asked.

"Okay," Kandagawa replied, and looked at the pages

Mano was sharing with her. The comic was about young men gambling, and Kandagawa couldn't understand the appeal. Mano kept on turning the pages, though, so she pretended to be following along.

, The windows were dark. The train passed through what were known as bedtowns, and each time it pulled into a station, a cool wind blew in through the open doors. Kandagawa's feet grew cold.

After a while, they got to the end of the comics section, and then came the pin-ups. Girls of around twenty years old wearing bikinis. It was that peculiarly Japanese brand of infantile sexiness.

There were about seven girls in total, so Kandagawa guessed that the idea was that readers enjoyed choosing the one they desired most. There was the party girl, the tomboy, the princess, the older-sister type, . . .

Mano was holding the photos out to her as if he thought nothing of it, so Kandagawa decided, somewhat mean-spiritedly, to play a game with him.

"Which is your favorite?"

"Ummm . . ."

"On the count of three, we point our fingers at the one we like best. Okay?"

"Okay."

"One, two, three . . ."

Both Kandagawa and Mano pointed to the same photo. It was a quiet-looking girl with straight black hair, who looked like she was somehow not entirely of this world.

"Snap," said Mano.

"Snap. Okay, turn over."

Mano turned the page to reveal a different selection of girls.

"Okay, same thing with these. One, two, three . . ."

Once again, they both pointed to the same girl. She had short hair, and a serious, childish face. So this was the kind of girl that Mano liked. Perhaps he was going to be pursuing twenty-year-olds for the rest of his life. It was a pretty gross thought, but then that was just how Mano was.

Kandagawa remembered the photographs of Yuko Ogura that she'd found on his computer when she sneaked a look.

But Kandagawa was herself no longer a girl like that. She was performing a job that carried considerable responsibility, and she was in total control of her own life. She was a grown woman.

When the two of them parted at Shibuya, Mano said, "It feels sad to say goodbye."

"Yeah," said Kandagawa, without feeling.

"Take care," Mano said, and then he reached out and patted Kandagawa on her head.

Kandagawa flinched — she couldn't help it. Her current boyfriend was older than she was, but he would never dream of patting a woman on her head. When he stood close by her, it was out of a sense of respect and admiration, and when he offered her his hand, it was because he viewed her as a kindred spirit to navigate his way through the world with. Mano was the same age as Kandagawa, but — come to think of it — he often used to pat her head. At the time she didn't mind it. In fact, it must have pleased her. But now that she had some kind of social confidence, having her head patted was an insult. It made her nauseous. A wave of disgust toward Mano rose up in her.

"Bye," she said, and waved. She walked away and did not look back.

When she got back to her apartment, she took off her coat, and then remembered the stone that she'd picked up in the vacant lot, which was still in her pocket. It was a white pebble, about the size of a peanut. She'd chosen it because it had looked somehow pure. She held it under the fluorescent light, and stared at it. It still had traces of soil on it. Unsure whether stones were combustible or non-combustible, she hesitated for a while. Then she threw it in with the non-combustible rubbish.

Lose Your Private Life

Terumi Yano went to see an author give a talk. Yano was an author herself, but a relatively new one. She still had a lot to learn.

The author stood at the podium, smoothly expounding on the novel. Yano listened very carefully and took notes. She realised that digesting new ideas on the spot wasn't her forte, and she didn't have much confidence that she understood what was being said.

After the talk, the question and answer session began. A delicately built man sitting in the middle of the front row immediately raised his hand. "My field is contemporary music," he began, "and there, I feel that the way that people listen to a piece depends largely on whether or not they have a prior understanding of musical theory. I suppose a person could cultivate a receptivity for contemporary music simply by studying musical theory. But what really fascinates me is the question of whether it's possible for a so-called outsider, who has no interest in music and doesn't understand the discourse surrounding it, to listen to a piece and appreciate its worth in the same way as somebody who is fully aware of musical theory. Do you think that question applies in a similar way to writing? I suppose I'm asking whether or not readers perceive things differently depending on whether they have a theoretical understanding of literature. People making contemporary classical music now actually require their listeners to have a grasp of musical theory, so it's becoming increasingly the case that this kind of music is appreciated by a very limited section of society, made up of people who share this particular understanding of music.

"You were saying that when you're writing a novel, wit doesn't matter to you if not all your readers understand it, that you're happy if just some of them do.

NAO-COLA YAMAZAKI

I was wondering if you could say more about this kind of 'division' within your readership. Because I have a kind of dream that art might provide a way for people with no theoretical knowledge to suddenly find themselves able to commune with people who do, but I've no idea if that's even possible . . ."

It should be noted here that this is the question as it was written up later by Yano, whose powers of comprehension are somewhat suspect, and so it may differ from the actual question that was asked.

In any case, as complicated as it was, the man's question intrigued the young author Terumi Yano, who wrote under the penname Waterumi Yano. She was currently in a tough phase with the novel she was in the middle of writing, by the title of *Friendship for Grown-Ups*, but she was already planning the next book that she would start once this one was finished, which she intended to call *A Musical Novel*. Yano didn't want her books to be something people read like essays in order to quench their thirst for knowledge or give them a mental workout. She wanted them to be looked at just as pieces of art, like music or paintings. But when she started thinking about what a novel was fundamentally, she grew confused, and then a bit panicky, and the hand holding her pen would freeze up.

When the event was over, there was an after-party, which Yano went to. In the *izakaya*, she found herself in a seat across from the man who had asked the intriguing question.

She had thought that he was younger than her, but she discovered that he was 28, the same age that she was, and that his name was Matsumoto. He said that he had read one of her books.

The two enjoyed speaking to one another, and exchanged email addresses. The after-party moved to another *izakaya* afterwards, and here they sat beside one another. wThey spoke about music and novels, but also about trivial things, like which celebrity had married whom, and which famous people were cute. Matsumoto said he thought Rina Ohta, the model for the clothing label Tsumori Chisato, was beautiful, and that he was a fan of the actress Yu Aoi. Yano admitted with a grin that she liked Tokui from the comedy duo Tutorial, who had won last year's M-1 stand-up competition, and that she also thought Goto from the stand-up act Jarujaru was funny.

"My knowledge of stand-up is pretty good," Matsumoto said. "That's one of the benefits of living in Kansai."

The Kansai region was the heart of Japan's stand-up comedy scene.

"You live in Kansai?"

"Yeah, in Kyoto. I stayed over at a friend's last night. I was planning to go back on the overnight bus tonight. I bought a ticket, but I was having so much fun I decided I'd go back tomorrow instead. Or today, I guess I should say. I'll get the first train back."

"Well, in that case, let's stay out until it's time for the first train."

"Great idea."

Yano was beginning to feel that she liked Matsumoto, so she felt a bit set back by the discovery that he lived in Kyoto. But they were grown-ups, after all. The distance wasn't so far as to prevent them from getting to know one another. I can go and visit him in Kyoto, she thought.

"I like Tsumori Chisato's clothes," Yano said. "I've got quite a few pieces of hers."

"I'm sort of envious. I've always wanted one of those brochures with Rina Ohta in, but, as a man, I'm too embarrassed to go into the shop."

Matsumoto had majored in conducting at music college. He had studied in France for a while, and was now devoting himself to contemporary classical music in Kyoto, where he was originally from. He was working part-time to pay his way.

"What does studying conducting involve? Do you have to learn about musical theory and study harmony and things like that?"

"Yes, pretty much... I don't know really how to explain it in simple terms, but basically, contemporary music grew out of earlier classical music, and you need a firm understanding of musical theory to write it, and even to enjoy it. So there aren't many people around creating it, and there's not much demand for it from listeners either."

"Do you use those theoretical methods in order to compose, then?"

"No, when I'm composing I forget about theory entirely, and just write."

The two of them left the bar in time for the first train. They parted at the station with a wave.

The next day, Matsumoto sent Yano a text message.

"I enjoyed myself talking with you yesterday. I come to Tokyo quite often, so I'll let you know the next time I'm planning a visit. Perhaps we could go out for dinner together. I'd like to play you some contemporary music."

Yano was delighted. She replied, "Yes, let's definitely have dinner!"

The two continued to exchange emails and texts. The one thing that bothered Yano was that, at the end of his emails, Matsumoto would always write: "Please write back if it's convenient. If you're too busy, though, I don't mind if you don't respond." It seemed like he assumed that she, being a writer, was constantly busy, but the words "I don't mind if you don't respond" made her feel weird.

About a month later, Matsumoto announced that he was coming to Tokyo, and the two of them arranged to meet for dinner. Yano found it odd, though, when Matsumoto wrote in his email, "I'm worried you'll be bored if we just have dinner, so I'll bring some DVDs or books with me." Was he

thinking that she would be more interested in reading
a book than in having dinner with him? Just because she
was a writer? The idea that he would think that about her
made her feel a bit sad.

Yano met Matsumoto at the station near her apartment,
and they went off to a yakitori restaurant. They drank
beer and ate skewers of grilled chicken.
It was fun, but their conversation didn't quite flow as
well as she'd hoped it would. Matsumoto kept talking
about symbols the whole time. He was trying to explain
to her about symbolisation as a means of interpretation,
and then about communication where language served
a symbolic function, but it wasn't easy for Yano to
understand, and she found herself feeling lost.

She managed to blurt out that she really liked him,
but even after that he carried on talking about his
theories of symbols. Still, even if she was unable to
follow their conversation entirely, Yano was glad just
to have met somebody that she liked for the first time in
ages, and felt quite content.

As a present, Matsumoto gave Yano a book called
Enlightenment for the Wicked, written by Shigesato Itoi,
a writer and game designer, and Takaaki Yoshimoto, a
poet and philosopher who was also the father of Banana
Yoshimoto. He also brought her the DVD *Near Equal –
Daido Moriyama*.

"There's a whole series of *Near Equal* documentaries,
right?"

"Yeah."

"I've got the one about Makoto Aida. I'm a really big
fan of his paintings."

"Yes, I like him a lot too."

Back in her apartment, Yano showed Matsumoto the DVD
she had mentioned.

"I went to see Tomoka Shibasaki a while back. She came
to give a talk in Osaka."

"How was she?"

"Oh, she's really cute. I feel like she is very congruent with what she writes."

"Do you think I'm like that? Congruent?"

"I think it's too early for me to say."

For a while after that meeting, too, the pair exchanged emails and texts, and called each other on the phone. Yano had the most stressful period with *Friendship for Grown-Ups*, and it cheered her up immensely to receive messages from him saying "I hope your novel is progressing well."

The only thing that niggled was that his insistence on using such a formal tone with her. She wished that he would stop — not specifically for any romantic reason, but just as someone of a similar age who was supposedly her peer.

She sent him an SMS saying, "If you don't mind, how about we stop being so formal with one other?"

But he didn't reply, so she sent another one saying, "If you'd prefer not to, that's fine too."

This time, his reply came straightaway.

"OK. Let's ditch the formalities."

He started adding emoticons and photographs to the messages he sent on his phone. Silly little conversations followed like, "I'm about to go make some music with a couple of guys," with a photo attached of him carrying musical gear.

"Nice! I guess you musicians can all go out for drinks afterwards to celebrate? (smiley face)"

"Ha, we're actually just heading out for drinks now. (beer icon)"

"Wow, nice! (star, star, star)"

After a while, though, Matsumoto lapsed back into using more formal language. Yano really wanted him to call her Teru or Teru-chan, like her friends did, rather than calling her by her penname, Waterumi, as he did now.

She thought that would be a good place to start from, and so she deliberately signed off her emails with Terumi. Yet, Matsumoto's replies always began with "Dear Waterumi."

Yano felt really disappointed by this, but she was at least certain that her novels were far more important to her than her love life was, and had no doubt that she would be left with far more regret if she slacked off on her work than if she messed up a relationship, so she decided to give up the project of having him call her Teru-chan. Her way of thinking became more and more calculating, and she began to feel that a relationship didn't have to be a burden so long as it helped her with her work. She even wrote to Matsumoto, "I'm really struggling with my writing at the moment. Will you send me a good luck message?"

Matsumoto replied, "I'm not an expert on novels at all, but I for one hope that you carry on writing. I'm wishing you the best of luck."

Feeding off these words of encouragement, Yano persevered with the book.

About a month after that, Matsumoto sent Yano a message saying that he was coming to Tokyo again to see a play: Oriza Hirata's *Tokyo Notes*. Yano replied saying she'd like go along with him.

"Okay, sure," Matsumoto said.

"Shall I get the tickets?"

"No, that's okay. I'll do it."

When Yano asked if he would send the ticket to her, she got a stiff reply that read: "With regular post, there's no insurance on the item. Maybe it would be wiser to use registered post or similar. What would you prefer?"

Yano felt really disappointed. She responded very simply, "Just send it by normal post, please."

After sending the message, though, she had a change of heart, and called Matsumoto up. Her mouth opening and closing like a goldfish, Yano somehow managed to get

her words out. "Um, so, I sent you that message before,
asking you if you could send me the ticket, but actually,
I was thinking, could we just meet up before the play
starts and I get it from you then?"

"Yes. That was what I was envisioning all along,"
said Matsumoto.

"The thing is, I get really nervous when I have to
meet people. So I was thinking that it would be better
to get the ticket from you first and just go to my seat
and meet you there. Last time when we met, I was really
nervous when I saw you standing in front of the train
station, but I couldn't pluck up the courage to go up to
you. I had to wander around for five minutes before
I managed it. You were standing there reading and didn't
notice me at all."

"Ahhh, that often happens to me. When I start reading,
I stop being able to hear the sounds going on around me."

"Oh, really, wow . . ."

"Anyway, that's beside the point. Let's meet up before,
I'll have your ticket, then we can go watch
the play."

"Okay."

The last time he had come to Tokyo, Matsumoto had
stayed in Yano's room, but she didn't know what that
meant. Yano would only sleep in a room with a member of
the opposite sex whom she was interested in. But that
was just Yano, and the same didn't necessarily apply to
everyone. Matsumoto might operate according to totally
different principles.

With that in mind, she decided in advance what she
would say to him, before the play started, the moment
they sat down in their seats: "Why don't you stay over
at my place tonight? You'd be more than welcome. I really
like you, you know. What do you think?"

Then they would watch the play feeling very awkward.

Yano was waiting eagerly in front of Komaba-Tōdaimae

station. When Matsumoto appeared, at exactly the time
that they had arranged to meet, she found herself
unable to speak. She licked her dry lips as they walked
toward the theatre. Sitting in their seats before the
performance started, it didn't seem at all the right
moment to say what she wanted to say, and her courage
buckled. She finally managed to come out with the words
she had prepared after the play was over, as they
were walking to the station. Matsumoto's response was
pretty vague.

They had Okinawan food for dinner, and then went to
Yano's room. The next morning, Yano made an omelette for
breakfast, along with miso soup and salad. As they ate,
they watched Aiko Kaito present the weather forecast on
Fuji TV's morning TV programme.

And yet, when Yano listened to the words that
Matsumoto actually said, it seemed as though he had no
intention of going out with her. Still they continued
emailing and calling one other regardless. Yano was
grateful just to have someone to offer her encouragement
with her novel.

So Yano continued working on *Friendship for Grown-Ups*.
She knew that it wasn't only Matsumoto who she had to
support her and her writing — she also had her friends
and family and editors, not to mention her readers.

The situation with Matsumoto was playing on her
mind, though, so Yano decided to go and visit him. When
she asked by email if it would be okay, his reply was
enthusiastic, and so Yano decided on a weekend when she
thought she would have already submitted the manuscript
for her novel, and made plans to travel to Kyoto.

However, after she booked her train, there were
numerous rounds of changes to the novel, and the deadline
was extended until just before the print deadline,
meaning that the weekend in question now fell before the
final submission date for the manuscript.

Yano calculated. She would be able to work on her book on the bullet train and in the hotel. Having dinner with Matsumoto would take three hours or so, and she could work on her book after. Better still, she could just make sure that it was in good shape already by that time. She wasn't going to become a good writer just by sitting at her desk and reading her words over and over. It's good to do things like this from time to time, Yano thought to herself as she stepped onto the Nozomi bullet train with a spring in her step.

Matsumoto came to meet her at the station near his apartment.

In his room, Matsumoto played Yano some contemporary music. It was a piece he had written himself.

The beat started, and then there were some bizarre mewling sounds.

"Is this tuning up?"

"Yes, very good."

"This is part of the music?"

"That's right."

There was the sound of voices talking, like at a bar, then a high-pitched bleeping noise.

"This is all very new to me, this kind of music, but I have the feeling that I understand the impetus to include these kinds of noises."

"I'm happy to hear that."

Then Matsumoto turned off the music, although the piece hadn't yet finished.

"Is this making you embarrassed?" Yano asked.

"Well spotted," said Matsumoto. He had turned red all the way to his earlobes.

It was fun until the evening. While they were out drinking in a bar that night, they got into a big argument. It was Yano's fault. Perhaps because the alcohol had gone to her head a bit or something, she found herself getting argumentative.

"Are you only interested in seeing me because I'm an author?"

"Why do you say that?"

"The only thing you ever ask me about is my novels."

"But you talk about books all the time yourself, and you ask me lots of questions about my music."

"I want to have a relationship with you."

"Having relationships isn't really my forte."

"I want to talk about other things than just books. I want it to be like we're just two people, talking. To just talk about unimportant things, whatever comes into our heads, you know?"

"You didn't like it when I talked about books?"

"I thought . . . It's like, the novels I write are sometimes about sex and things, so I thought maybe you thought that I was easy or something, but actually the real me isn't really like that at all. I haven't had all that many serious relationships."

"I don't really understand."

"I mean, I'm just a normal girl, is what I guess I'm trying to say."

"Do I seem to you like the sort of person who would get off from sleeping with a celebrity?"

"No, I don't mean —"

"Weren't you interested in me just because I was a musician anyway?"

"No, not at all. I like you for who you are, I'm interested in you, romantically," she said, but as she said it she was thinking to herself, he's probably right. Yano wanted to write a novel about music, so she had been showering him with questions about it.

"I think we should stop seeing each other. I don't feel like I'll be able to talk to you as I did before."

"I'm really sorry about the way it all turned out." Yano bowed her head.

"No, no, it's not you." Matsumoto looked uncomfortable.

"I guess I'll see you around."
"I'll still read your books."
"Okay."

Yano got into a taxi and waved Matsumoto goodbye. Downtown Kyoto looked a lot like Tokyo, she thought. There were cars, and the roads gleamed, and there were lots of restaurants and hotels.

Yano stayed the night in a budget hotel catering to business travellers, and then, the next morning, got back on the bullet train. She sat in her seat and, for a while after the train pulled away from the station, found herself unable to think of anything. Her eyes aimlessly followed the scenery sliding along above outside the window.

After half an hour or so, she pulled out the printout of her manuscript from her bag. Yano's process when writing her books was as follows: she would write her first draft by hand in a notebook, type this up, and print it out. She would read the draft through and make corrections by hand. Then she would type these corrections up, print the draft out again, and repeat, again and again.

Now three days before the due date, her draft was already complete. Still, she wanted to check it again, so she sat there, passing her eyes over it.

Yano had not gone to Kyoto because she was in love with Matsumoto. There had been an ulterior motive for her trip: the thought that she would be better able to write books about love affairs if she had one herself, better able to write about music if she spoke about it with someone. She felt the pressing need to gain experience of all the things life had to offer, and she knew that if she sat in front of her desk all day she would just grow increasingly isolated and self-reliant. Yano was cruel and inhumane, and she had wanted to use Matsumoto for her writing. That was what she thought to herself.

"Are you crying?" said the middle-aged red-faced man sitting beside her. He was drinking a can of beer and reading a weekly magazine read by middle-aged men with a woman on the cover.

"Mmm," Yano nodded, and dabbed under her eyes with her fingers.

"You shouldn't cry," said the man.

"Mmm," said Yano.

"Are you a writer?"

"Mm."

"Good luck with that."

"Mm."

Yano's replies grew more and more curt, and then she turned to face the window. How had the man known she was a novelist, she wondered. Had he been sneaking a look? You wouldn't usually make that assumption just because somebody had a sheaf of paper with them. There was no way he could have known she were an author unless he'd been reading her work on the sly.

Yano brought the pages up close to her face, sheltering them from view, and continued making her corrections.

When she got back to her apartment, she inputted the changes into the file on her computer.

Then she printed the novel out again, and with the stack of paper in hand, went to an all-night diner nearby. She drank green tea, which she dispensed from the self-service counter, and read through her novel once again.

Even if I can't stop crying, and can't eat or sleep from now on, at least I can still do my work, she thought to herself.

Yano was twenty-eight years old, and had gotten to the stage where, whatever the situation, she found it simpler and easier just to do whatever it was she was supposed to do, to smile pleasantly to anyone she had to meet for work. There was a certain degree of sadness to

that fact. Yano was now an adult. She would never return
to the days of wanting to take time off school when she
had her heart broken.

The next day, Matsumoto sent Yano an email.

"Dear Waterumi, You told me honestly how you felt, but
I didn't share my feelings with you. I understand that
was an unacceptable way to behave. Please don't think I am
taking this lightly. I know that I hurt you. I think that
what you were saying was that you wanted me to see you
not as a novelist, but as a person. But I don't think that
I can think of someone whose novels I've read as anything
but a novelist. Goodbye."

His writing goodbye at the end was really weird, she
thought. Why did people bother saying 'goodbye', anyway?
'Hello' made sense. It was something you said to someone
you'd met to show them that you were interested in
getting to know them better. But 'goodbye'? Why on earth
would you write something like that when it was crystal
clear to both of you that things were over, and you would
never meet again?

Yano's emotional swings were much more violent when
it came to her love life than they were toward her work.
She felt a hundred times happier if somebody told her she
was pretty than she did if they said her books were good.
She cried a hundred times more tears when she had her
heart broken than when someone criticised her novels.
Yet that was just emotion. She could survive without
love, no problem.

Her raison d'être lay with her work. It was when she
failed at work-related things that she felt herself
becoming less herself. What shook her to her very core
was not being dumped, but the feeling of having no
confidence in her books. Her books were a part of her.

Yano sent off the manuscript for *Friendship for Grown-
ups*, and managed to pull herself back together.

She decided that she would do away with the idea of

having a private life. She would make her entire self
a public entity. It was no longer possible to separate
herself-as-novelist from her true self.

Yano got together with her friends from university,
and went for drinks.

"Teru-chan, I want your autograph!" said Mutoh, so Yano
wrote WATERUMI on his copy of her book.

"Draw that ghost guy that you always used to draw in
university," said Mano, so Yano drew the cartoon ghost
for him.

"There was I thinking you'd gone and become a
celebrity, but when we're all together like this, I can't
think of you as Waterumi at all. You're just the same
old Teru-chan," said Kandagawa, and Yano found herself in
danger of crying with joy. Kandagawa was right. Inside,
she was just the same Teru-chan. People who met her from
now on, though, would never see her as Teru-chan. She had
already become Waterumi.

She had always absolutely hated it when her friends
jokingly spoke about her as though she were some kind
of figure of authority. People she knew often said things
like, "Wow, you're so famous now!" or "I saw that you've
been nominated for that prize! Good luck!" or "Your book's
being made into a movie, right? That's so cool!" She knew
that these people were just using the little knowledge
they had about her in order to offer her praise, so there
was no point taking them literally. People were just
trying to express encouragement and support for her and
her writing. Nonetheless, these kinds of compliments
always left Yano with mixed feelings.

The only thing I want to do is to write. I didn't become a writer because I wanted to be famous. But I'm trying, because the more my name and my face are known, the more likely I am to sell more books.

I hate it when people say things that suggest that books are somehow a less important art form than movies. So I want people to stop saying things that suggest that having a book of mine made into a movie is more impressive than getting it published in the first place. But I want to sell more books, so I allow the movies to be made.

I don't write books out of the desire for recognition. But I want to continue being able to make a living as a writer, so I would consider myself lucky if I received a prestigious prize.

There were so many things that she wanted to say, in fact, that they came frothing out of her, like the swathes of foam that appear when you squeeze a sponge.

I know that everyone works hard, whatever kind of job they do. People give me more attention because my profession is more noticeable, but I have the same kind of life as everyone else.

I think finding someone you think is so special that you want to marry them is a far more incredible feat than winning a literary prize.

Building human relationships is a more amazing thing than creating prose.

These were the things that went through Yano's head, but she found it hard to come out with them.

Instead, she would respond with the sort of thing she thought people were expecting, like, "Thanks! I'm doing the best I can."

What it all boiled down to was the fact that she hadn't managed to make him fall in love with her. She had been rejected, plain and simple. But it had been a fruitful experience for her as a writer, and that was a good thing.

One day, about two months later, Yano went to eat at a *soba* restaurant with a male friend about thirty years older than her. She had her *soba* with grated yam, and he had his with shrimp, and they shared a bottle of beer.

Yano spoke to her friend about the whole thing, saying, "I got my heart broken by a man who liked my novels but didn't like me, but of course I'm a separate entity from my novels, and so I can't get close to the people who like my books. I fall in love because I think that unless I fall in love I won't be able to write properly, but the things I write are a thousand times more attractive than I myself am so nobody ever likes me as a person, but I'm going to give my life up to writing novels, so it doesn't matter."

Her friend listened, nodding along, and then told her what he thought: "But aren't you kind of missing the point by saying to somebody, 'You only like my novels, you don't like me!' Imagine if you were with a guy who went on about how cute your eyebrows were. Would you tell him, 'You only like me for my eyebrows!?'"

"Hahaha!"

"I think it's the same with novels. Your novels are a part of you, so isn't it okay if he likes them? It doesn't really matter what first draws someone to you."

It struck her that she would never again have a love affair as plain old Terumi Yano. From now on, she would have her love affairs as Waterumi. If she couldn't write, then there was no point in being alive. Her life was what it was because she wrote.

Yano opened up her notebook, and started on the first draft of *A Musical Novel*.

About the Project

Keshiki is a series of chapbooks showcasing the work of some of the most exciting writers working in Japan today, published by Strangers Press, part of the UEA Publishing Project.

Each story is beautifully translated and presented as an individual chapbook, with a design inspired by the text.

Keshiki is a unique collaboration between University of East Anglia, Norwich University of the Arts, and Writers' Centre Norwich, funded by the Nippon Foundation.

Supported by